Discovery at Dawn

Written by Maria Grace Datcno, FSP
Illustrated by Paul Cunningham

Pauline
BOOKS & MEDIA
Boston

Library of Congress Cataloging-in-Publication Data

Dateno, Maria Grace.
  Discovery at dawn / written by Maria Grace Dateno, FSP ; illustrated by
Paul Cunningham.
    pages cm. -- (Gospel time trekkers ; 6)
  Summary: Siblings Hannah, Caleb, and Noah, aged six through ten,
travel to Jerusalem at the time of Jesus's death and resurrection, hoping
that this will be the time they actually see Him.
  ISBN-13: 978-0-8198-1895-9
  ISBN-10: 0-8198-1895-X
  [1. Time travel--Fiction. 2. Brothers and sisters--Fiction. 3. Jesus Christ-
-Fiction. 4. Christian life--Fiction. 5. Jerusalem--History--1st century--Fic-
tion.] I. Cunningham, Paul (Paul David), 1972- illustrator. II. Title.
  PZ7.D2598Dis 2014
  [Fic]--dc23

                            2013016835

The Scripture quotations contained herein are from the *New Revised
Standard Version Bible: Catholic Edition*, copyright © 1989, 1993, Division
of Christian Education of the National Council of the Churches of Christ
in the United States of America. Used by permission. All rights reserved.

Cover design by Mary Joseph Peterson, FSP
Cover and interior art by Paul Cunningham

"P" and PAULINE are registered trademarks of the Daughters of St. Paul.

Published by Pauline Books & Media, 50 Saint Pauls Avenue, Boston,
MA 02130-3491

Printed in the U.S.A

DAD KSEUSAHUDNHA5-261065 1895-X

www.pauline.org

Pauline Books & Media is the publishing house of the Daughters of St. Paul,
an international congregation of women religious serving the Church with
the communications media.

3 4 5 6 7 8 9   20 19 18 17 16

*To Jane Palladino and Doris Gillis,
in gratitude for their
constant prayers.*

Contents

Chapter One

Trek to the City

"Not that one, Caleb!" said Noah.

"We have to give some good ones," I said. "You can't give only the *yucky* vegetables to the poor."

Mom had told me, my sister Hannah, and my brother Noah to fill a bag with canned goods for the food drive at church the next day. My little brother Noah only wanted to give the beans and beets. He didn't want me to put any corn in the bag because he likes it. But he's only six, so what can you expect?

"All right," he sighed. "Give them one can."

I took it and put it in the bag.

"Wait! Not those!" I said as Hannah put two cans of mini ravioli in the bag.

"Caleb, you just said we have to give some good stuff. We can't just give the stuff we don't like."

"He meant good vegetables," said Noah. "Not ravioli. I like that, too."

"Mom can get more," said Hannah. "It's not like you're never going to have any ever again."

Hannah's eleven and sometimes acts like she's grown-up.

"But I wanted it for lunch," said Noah. "Those are the last two cans."

Noah and I looked at each other. I was planning on ravioli for lunch, too. Mom let us have it on Saturdays. But I thought of some little kid who would be happy when his mom came back from the food pantry with ravioli.

"Noah, let's give them one. You can have the other one for lunch," I said.

Noah looked at me and sighed again. "No, let's give them both. We can get more."

"Okay, I think this is enough. Let's show Mom," said Hannah.

We got up and Hannah and I each took a handle of the bag. We had only gone a few steps when it happened. We began moving in slow motion, as if the air had become thick. And then, a few seconds later, we were standing still. The bag was gone. The air was back to normal, except for the smell. It really stunk!

"Yay! Yay!" yelled Noah, jumping up and down. "It happened! It happened! We're here!"

Noah's T-shirt and jeans had disappeared. He was now wearing a tan-colored robe that went down to his knees. It was tied with a rope belt. It didn't look odd, though. Hannah and I were wearing the same things, except hers had decoration around the neck. They're called tunics.

Hannah and I looked at each other and smiled. We were back in the time of Jesus! This had already happened to us five times, but we were always amazed when it did. We couldn't figure out how to tell when it was going to happen.

We looked around and saw that we were standing in a dirty alley. It was smelly because of the piles of garbage lying around. A few feet away from us, a dog was eating something off the ground.

"This time," I said, "we *are* going to see Jesus! I know we are!"

"We've been so close," said Hannah.

"Rrrrrrruff!" I turned to see the dog snap at Noah.

"Watch it, Noah," Hannah said. "Don't try to pet a dog like that. You don't know if it's friendly."

"I just went to look," said Noah. "I didn't pet him."

"Yuck, what's he eating?" I said.

"I don't know, but he doesn't have a collar," said Noah.

"Noah, I don't think dog collars have been invented yet," said Hannah.

For some reason that made us laugh and we all stood there laughing until the dog started barking at us. We stopped and it ran off down the alley.

"I don't remember it being so stinky when we were here before," I said.

"Well, maybe we're not in a place we've been. We've never come back to the same place twice," said Hannah.

In my head, I counted back over the towns we had been to: Bethlehem, Cana, Gennesaret, Capernaum, and Jericho.

"Come on! Let's go look around!" said Noah.

As we walked down the alley to the larger street, I thought how funny it was that we acted like this was completely normal. The first time it happened, we were confused and kind of scared. But now, it was just a great adventure.

We had given up trying to make it happen, but I still thought that if we could figure out how it worked, we could come back whenever we wanted. The neat thing was, it didn't take any time. I mean, we were always gone for two days, but each time we came back, only a few minutes had gone by in our time.

"Wow," said Noah when we reached the street.

Wow was right. This was definitely a bigger city than any we had been in before. There were houses crowded close together in every direction. They were made of stone and most seemed to have two stories.

"Look at that!" Noah said. We looked where he was pointing and saw in the distance the high wall of a building. It was up on a hill all by itself, so we could see it from where we stood.

"Yeah, this really is a big city," I said. "Where do you think we are, Hannah?" Hannah was the one who spent the most time looking at the maps in our Bible at home.

"I think," Hannah said slowly, "maybe this is Jerusalem."

Chapter Two

Jonathan and David

"Jerusalem?" asked Noah. "That's where Jesus was. I mean, last time, when we were in Jericho, they said he had just left for Jerusalem, right?"

"Yes," said Hannah. "If he's still here, we need to find out quickly where he is. It's going to be harder to find our way around this big city."

"We always have until the 'third day'," said Noah.

We had found out the first time we came that the people here said "the third day" to mean two days later. They counted it like the day itself was the first day, then the second, then the third.

"Okay," I said. "He's got to be here! Let's just ask the first person we meet."

A woman came by, carrying one basket on her head and another on her arm. She was walking quickly, and seemed to be thinking about something. She didn't look at us until I said something.

"Excuse me," I said. "Could you tell us if this is the city of Jerusalem?"

The woman stopped and stared at me, then at Noah, then Hannah.

"You have very strange-looking hair, so you must be from somewhere far away!" she said.

Almost everyone here had brown or black hair. Noah and I had short, straight, sand-colored hair. At least Hannah's was brownish, so she didn't stand out as much. We just looked at her, waiting for the answer to our question.

"Yes, of course this is Jerusalem!" the woman said.

"Oh, good," said Noah.

"I must be getting home. And I would offer you a place to stay if we had any. But we have pilgrims who have come for the feast filling our entire house."

"That's all right," said Hannah. "Just one more question. Do you know if the teacher Jesus from Galilee is here in Jerusalem?"

"Why, yes, he is," she said. "My husband told me he saw him a few days ago. He came with a large crowd and they were all excited and were cheering him as he rode into the city."

"Do you know where he is staying?" I asked.

"No, I do not. I am sorry I cannot help you," she said. "I must be going."

"Thank you so much!" said Hannah.

"Well, that was helpful, but we need to find out where he is," I said.

"There aren't many people around," said Noah. "I wonder why."

"Well, it seems to be around noon," said Hannah. "So maybe they're inside having lunch."

We walked down several streets. There were lots of houses, and we saw some people from a distance, but didn't pass very many.

One man walking quickly didn't even look at us when we said hello. Another woman wouldn't stop. She just said sorry, she had to be getting home, like the first one.

Then we came around a corner and saw some children—two boys and two younger girls. The boys both had curly black hair, with headbands tied around their heads. One was a little taller than the other. The girls looked exactly alike. They had long wavy black hair. All of them wore tunics like ours.

The kids had a little puppy with them, and they were throwing a stick for it to fetch.

"Hello," one of the boys said. He looked about my age. "My name is Jonathan."

"I'm Caleb, and this is my sister Hannah, and my brother Noah."

"Ha, ha! Noah is here, David! Soon it will be raining, right?" Jonathan said to the other boy, who laughed too. "Welcome! This is my brother David," he said to us. "And those are his sisters, Rachel and Elizabeth."

"And this is our dog, Sniffer," said David, rubbing the puppy's stomach as it rolled over onto its back.

"Well, you know he is not really *our* dog," Jonathan said. "When he gets bigger, he will not want to play with us anymore. He will be wild and nasty like the rest of them. That is what always happens, right?"

"He will not be nasty," said one of the girls. I didn't know if it was Rachel or Elizabeth.

"Abba says dogs are helpful because they eat the garbage in the streets," said the other girl.

We had learned on our other adventures that "Abba" means "Dad" and "Imma" means "Mom."

Noah went over to pet the puppy.

"Are you twins?" he asked the two little girls.

"Yes," they said at the same time.

"We are five," said Rachel or Elizabeth.

"How old are you?" the other asked.

"I'm six," said Noah.

"We have a new baby brother, too," said

the first twin. "He was born yesterday. His name is Jacob."

"You look our age, Caleb," said Jonathan. "I am nine and David is eight."

"I'm nine," I said. "And Hannah's eleven."

"You are tall for your age," said Jonathan. "Both of you. And your hair is strange!"

"Do you live here?" Hannah asked, ignoring his comment about our hair.

"Yes, we live here in the lower city," said David.

"My father and mother serve in the house of Reuben the banker, in the upper city. I also work in the kitchen there, when Reuben is having a dinner or many guests," said Jonathan.

"My father is a brickmaker," said David.

"What?" I said. "I thought you said you were brothers?"

"Our fathers are brothers," said Jonathan. "So we are brothers, too, right?"

"No, you're cousins," I said. "Not brothers."

"Oh, well, it's the same thing," Jonathan shrugged.

I was surprised he didn't seem to think it made any difference.

"Caleb," said Hannah, leaning toward me, "remember how the Bible talks about the brothers and sisters of Jesus? They used those words to mean different kinds of relatives."

"Oh," I said.

"We heard that Jesus is here in Jerusalem," Hannah said to the boys. "Do you know where we can find him?"

"Do you mean Jesus, the teacher everyone talks about?"

"Yes, that one!" said Noah.

"The one who tells stories, right?"

"Yes," said Hannah.

"The one who heals and even raises people from the dead?"

"Yes!" I said. "Do you know where he is staying?"

Jonathan and David smiled at each other.

"Yes, we do!"

Chapter Three

Follow That Man

"So, where is Jesus staying?" I asked.

"In the upper room at the house where my father works," said Jonathan. "It is not far from here."

"What is an 'upper room'?" asked Noah.

Jonathan pointed to a house nearby. It had a second floor and a small stairway going up the side of the house to get to it.

"Like that one in our house, except that it is much bigger because the house is much bigger," explained Jonathan.

"Our house has one, too," said David,

pointing to the house across the street from Jonathan's.

"Would you like to hear the story of how Jesus came there yesterday?" asked Jonathan.

"Yes!" said Noah. We all loved when people told us stories of Jesus, but Noah got the most excited about it.

"As you heard," said Jonathan, "David's mother had a baby yesterday. The midwife sent me to get my mother, who was at work with my father, in the house of Reuben. The baby was sick and David's mother was sick, too. So she needed help. When I came to the house, my mother was just about to fetch water from the well in the square. She was worried about David's mother and wanted to go immediately to help. So my father told her to go quickly, and he took the water jar and went to fill it.

"But when my father was returning, he saw two men walking slowly and looking around. They were strangers, but that was not surprising. There are many visitors in Jerusalem for the feast. But then, as he went toward the house, they followed him."

"Are you sure they weren't just going the same way he was going?" I asked.

"He saw them coming behind him—he saw them twice as he turned a corner and looked back. They were whispering to each other and looking at him. He walked more quickly and got to the house and closed the door, wondering who they were and what he should do."

"Did he call the police?" asked Noah.

"What?"

"Nothing. Never mind," I said. "What happened after that?"

"My father thought he should tell Reuben, the master of the house, but immediately there was a knocking at the door," continued Jonathan. "My father opened the door and one of the men said, 'The Teacher asks where his guest room is.'"

"What does that mean?" asked Noah.

"The Teacher is Jesus!" said David.

"Of course Reuben let him use the upper room," said Jonathan. "David and I were there when Jesus came with his disciples to stay that evening."

"Did your father and Reuben know Jesus already?" asked Hannah.

"Of course," said Jonathan. "I do not know how Reuben knows him, but Abba has listened to him teaching in the Temple whenever he was in Jerusalem. And he has seen his disciples with him. But he just didn't recognize the two who were following him last night."

"Oh," said Noah. "But I don't get why the two disciples followed your father."

"It turns out that Jesus told them to go into the city and follow a man carrying a water jar," said Jonathan.

"But how did they know which one to follow?" I asked.

David and Jonathan laughed.

"Men do not carry water jars," said David.

"It was only because my mother had to leave quickly to help David's mother that my father went to get the water from the well."

"Oh," said Noah. "But how did Jesus know your father would be doing that?"

"We do not know," said David. "But the teacher Jesus is very amazing. Somehow he knew."

"Let's go get something to eat," said Rachel or Elizabeth. I really couldn't tell them apart. "We can go to your house, Jonathan."

The house was kind of like the ones we had been in during our other adventures, except that it had the second floor.

We went into the house, and Jonathan introduced us to his older sister, Ruth.

"All of you, sit down and eat quickly," said Ruth. "I have much to do this afternoon. Imma is still helping your mother, David. I hope everything is all right."

Rachel and Elizabeth looked worried. David did, too.

"We only got to see our little brother one time," said Rachel or Elizabeth. "I think he is still sick."

"And Imma is sick, too," said the other one.

For lunch, we had bread and cheese. It was very good. Then Ruth sent us outside with handfuls of nuts. We ate them as we walked along.

"Why is it so dark?" asked Rachel or Elizabeth.

"Maybe it will rain," I said.

"Jonathan, do you know any more stories about Jesus?" asked Noah.

"Oh, I know one," said David.

"Let's hear it!" I said.

At that moment, we heard the sound of heavy footsteps from around the corner—like some men marching down the street. Jonathan and David stopped and turned to listen. Then they grabbed the hands of Rachel and Elizabeth.

"Come on!" said Jonathan. "Hide in here!"

Chapter Four

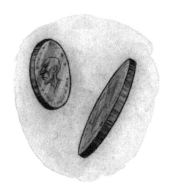

Soldiers and Coins

We all squeezed into a narrow space between two buildings. After a while we couldn't hear the sound of marching feet anymore.

"What was that about?" asked Hannah. "Who were we hiding from?"

"Soldiers, of course!" said David.

"Why do you hide from soldiers?" asked Noah.

Jonathan laughed, but I thought it was a good question.

"The Roman soldiers in this city are allowed to make anyone do any work for them," said

Jonathan. "They can grab you and say, 'Here, boy, do this or that.' And you have to do it, or you get in trouble."

"Not all of them are so mean," said Rachel or Elizabeth.

"You say that because they just smile at you. You have never been made to run a message or carry a load for them," said David.

"Well, now that they're gone, can you tell us your story about Jesus?" I asked.

"Yes," said David. "I was with my father in the Temple a few days ago. We saw a crowd of people and when we got closer, we realized that they were gathered around, listening to Jesus. Unfortunately, we missed most of what he was saying. We only heard the last part. He was talking about not acting like the scribes who show off all the time."

"What are scribes?" asked Noah.

"They are men who have studied a lot," said David. "They know a lot about the Law, which is good. But Jesus said not to be like them when they do things just to look good and get people to honor them.

"Anyway, that's what Jesus was talking about when we walked up and stood at the edge of the crowd. Then he got up and walked away. The crowd broke up and started leaving too. My father and I were disappointed that we had missed most of his teaching, so we followed him. Jesus went and sat down in another place. It was near where people were putting their offerings in the treasury."

"Putting their *what* into *what*?" I asked.

"They were giving money to the Temple," explained David. "Jesus sat there watching them. There were some people who put in a lot of money. They looked very proud of themselves for being so generous. The money made a lot of noise when it fell into the collection box.

"Then a widow went up. I could tell she was very poor."

Noah looked like he was about to ask a question, so I quickly said, "A widow is a woman whose husband has died. Like Leah, who we met on our last trip."

"Oh, yeah," said Noah.

"Well, this widow walked up and dropped two small coins in the treasury. They barely made a sound. Then she walked away.

"Jesus looked at his disciples who were nearby and said, 'This widow put in more than all the others.'"

"What?" I said. "Why did he say that?"

"I know. It does not seem to make sense, does it?" said David, smiling.

"How can two coins be more than lots of coins?" asked Noah.

"That is what I was thinking," said David. "But Jesus explained. He said that the other people gave a lot of money, but it was extra. After they gave the money, they still had plenty. But it was different for the widow. She had no extra. She only put in two coins, but that was everything she had.

"They gave some; she gave all. All is more than some."

Chapter Five

Voices in the Alley

"Wow," said Noah.

"Yeah, that was amazing," I said.

"Thank you, David," said Hannah. "That makes me want to be more generous with all the things I have!"

When David finished, I suddenly noticed how dark it had become.

"Now it is really dark," I said, "darker than if it were going to rain."

"I wonder if anyone knows what's going on, or why the sky is getting like this," said Jonathan.

"We could go toward the second quarter," said David. "There are probably people in the street talking about it."

"Rachel and Elizabeth, go home now," said Jonathan. "You are too young to be coming with us. Tell Ruth that we will be back before sunset."

"Noah is young, too! He should come with us," said Rachel or Elizabeth.

"The three of us have to stay together," I said before Noah could answer.

Rachel and Elizabeth went back to the house, and we set off down the street.

"Rachel said that would happen," said Noah. "She said David and Jonathan always send them home when they're going to have fun."

"How do you know Rachel said it and not Elizabeth? They look exactly alike," I said.

"No, they don't," said Noah. "Rachel has dimples when she smiles. Elizabeth's chin is rounder."

It was now getting dark like it was late evening, even though it was only one or two o'clock in the afternoon. There were more people in the streets than before, but everyone still seemed to be in a hurry.

"What's that?" asked Noah as we walked toward a big building up ahead on our right.

Jonathan explained that it was a stadium for sports.

"We don't go there," said David.

"And what's that?" asked Noah, pointing to the large building farther ahead on the hill that we had seen before.

"That's the Temple, of course," said Jonathan.

"Are we going to go up there?"

"No, you see the stairs up ahead, right? We could go up those and get into the Temple, but we want to look around a little. I want to hear what people are saying about this darkness," said Jonathan.

We continued past the huge staircase and down the street which led under an archway. The buildings were not as crowded here, and it wasn't quite as smelly.

"Let's go toward the marketplace," said David. "You can always get news there."

Jonathan and David seemed to know their way around pretty well. We all followed as they turned left into a much narrower street—more like an alley.

"We can cut through here and then take the next street up to the market," Jonathan explained. "If we go up the main one, we have to pass near some of the soldiers who are always posted in one part of the market, right, David?"

We walked by a dog eating something off the ground. He snarled at us and Noah jumped, but Jonathan and David didn't pay any attention to it.

As we walked farther into the alley, we heard voices. Jonathan stopped and motioned to us to stay still and quiet. He started sneaking forward, toward where the voices were coming from, and I followed a little behind him.

"What will we do?" a man's voice was saying. He sounded upset.

"I do not know, Andrew. I do not know," said another man. Then there was a noise that kind of sounded like he was crying.

"Will we be next, do you think?" asked Andrew. "They came for Jesus. Will the soldiers come looking for us?"

"I think they—" the man started to reply, but he stopped suddenly. He must have heard our footsteps. Or maybe I made a sound when I heard the name "Jesus."

"Who is there?" the man asked.

Jonathan and I didn't reply. I was hoping they would think they were imagining things, but there were some whispers and then the sound of the two men running off down the alley.

Chapter Six

Sad News

"Did you hear? They said something about Jesus," I said. "Let's follow them!"

We all ran down the alley and got a glimpse of them as they reached the street and turned left.

We turned, too, and saw them walking quickly up ahead, down a wide street. There was a very high wall behind the buildings on the right-hand side.

"Are they going toward the market?" Hannah asked.

"No, they're going the opposite direction.

The market and the Damascus gate are the other way," Jonathan replied.

We hurried to get closer to the two men, and at one point, one of them looked back and saw us. He poked the other, who also looked back. They whispered back and forth as they walked, and soon slowed down. Then they stopped walking and looked back at us.

"Why are you following us?" one of them asked.

"They are only children, Peter," said the other. That would be Andrew.

"I know they are children. I still want to know why they are following us and who sent them," said Peter.

"No one sent us," said Hannah.

"We are just trying to find out if anyone knows why the sky is so dark," I said.

"Wait," said Jonathan. "I know you, right?"

Peter and Andrew jumped. I didn't understand why they were so scared.

"You were staying in the upper room of Reuben the banker. My father works for him.

I did not recognize you at first in this darkness. I am Jonathan, and this is David."

"Oh, yes," said Peter. "I remember seeing you."

"I'm Caleb," I said. "My sister and brother and I are visitors."

"I'm Hannah."

"I'm Noah."

"It is nice to meet you, but we need to go now," said Peter.

"Are you in trouble?" asked Jonathan. "I can help you hide if you are in trouble or something."

"We are not in trouble!" said Peter, a little too loudly. "Why would you say that?"

"You were acting kind of scared," said David.

"Are you disciples of Jesus? We really want to see him. We've come so far. Can you tell us where he is?" asked Noah.

At that, Andrew put his hands over his face with a sob. Peter looked away and I think he was crying again, too.

"What's wrong?" asked Hannah.

"I feel sad, too," said Noah. "But I don't know why."

"It must be the darkness," said Jonathan. "It feels very heavy."

"You are too late to see Jesus!" Andrew sobbed. "He is dead, or soon will be."

"What? No!" I couldn't believe it. It couldn't be true!

"No, no, no!" said Noah. "We have to see him. All these trips and we were so close. Please!"

Hannah just stood there with her mouth open, looking like she was going to cry.

"Why is he dead?" asked David.

Andrew still stood with his hands over his face. Peter just shook his head. "It is hard to explain, and you children would not understand. You see, we—"

He didn't finish what he was going to say because at that moment we heard the sound of marching feet again. But it sounded like many more feet than last time.

We listened for a second, and then all of us started running, away from the soldiers and down a narrow street. It was very dark now, and there weren't many people.

Andrew and Peter were in front and we all followed them between some buildings. They stopped and leaned against the wall. We were all breathing hard.

"Are those the soldiers that killed Jesus?" asked Noah.

"No," said Andrew. "Or rather, yes, but they are not the only ones to blame."

"What do you mean by that?" said Peter angrily.

"We were there!" said Andrew, sounding angry, too. "Judas betrayed him right in front of us. What did we do? We ran away!" Then he turned to Jonathan. "And the people of this city, who have heard his teaching and seen his miracles—what did they do? They turned away! We are all to blame!" He stopped and covered his face with his hands again, and sobbed.

Noah was crying, too. Suddenly, the world seemed a very sad and scary place. I put my arms around Noah and moved closer to Hannah.

"We should go back home, right?" said Jonathan. "It must be getting close to sunset, even if we cannot see the sun."

"Yes, I want to see how my mother and baby brother are doing," said David.

"You will stay with us, too," said Jonathan to Hannah, Noah, and me.

"We must go back and see if the rest of our company has returned to the upper room," said Peter.

On the way, two other men came over to us and greeted Peter and Andrew.

"This is Thomas, and this is Matthew," Andrew said to us.

"I can't believe this," Hannah said to me. "Here are the apostles. We were so close to seeing Jesus!"

At Jonathan's house, Ruth gave us something to eat. I didn't even pay attention to what it was. Soon we lay down to sleep in a corner, trying to stay out of the way. I saw a man who must have been Jonathan's father. There seemed to be a lot going on, but I didn't even care to ask what. Jesus was dead. What else mattered?

Chapter Seven

An Empty Day

Right before I fell asleep, I remembered that Mary the mother of Jesus was there when he died. I wondered where she was—if she was staying in the upper room. I wanted to ask someone about it, but I was too tired.

When I woke up the next day, I felt like crying. It was funny because I felt like crying even before I remembered why I was sad.

I got up and saw that Hannah was helping Ruth prepare breakfast. It seemed that Jonathan's mom was still at David's house. I didn't know where everyone else was. Noah was still asleep, so I just sat there, wrapped in a blanket, feeling sad.

After breakfast, the three of us went out by ourselves. It was quiet. Not dark and heavy like the day before, but quiet and empty.

"Why isn't there anyone around?" asked Noah.

"Probably because it's the Sabbath—Saturday," said Hannah. "The Jewish people don't work or even travel very far on the Sabbath. It's a day of rest."

We walked down the street slowly. We weren't going anywhere. We didn't have anything to do. So we just walked to do something.

We reached the small square where there had been a market the day before, and it was completely empty.

"Hannah," said Noah, as we stood looking at nothing, "how did Jesus die?"

Hannah didn't answer right away. I thought to myself of what I remembered from the story in the Bible and the Stations of the Cross that we prayed at church during Lent.

Jesus was arrested, and then scourged and crowned with thorns. And then he carried the cross to Calvary. They nailed him to it, and he died after suffering a lot. They were so mean to him, but he didn't do anything back.

"Well, Noah," said Hannah. "You've seen a crucifix many times. That is how Jesus died."

"Where?" asked Noah, as we continued walking down the street.

"It must be pretty near here," said Hannah. "Just outside the city somewhere, but I don't know which direction."

"So, the night before last, Jesus and the apostles were in the upper room in Reuben's house," I said. "So that is where the Last Supper was."

"Wow, you're right," said Hannah. "And then after that they went to the Mount of Olives. That's somewhere outside the city, too."

"And that's where Jesus was arrested?" I said.

"Yes," said Hannah.

"I don't get it," said Noah. He looked so sad.

"What don't you get?" asked Hannah.

"Why did Jesus have to die?"

We all walked in silence for a while.

"I don't get it, either, Noah," Hannah said finally. "All I know is that he died because he loved us."

I thought of all the stories I knew about Jesus. I thought of how I talked to him when I prayed, and how he came to me in Holy Communion. I knew he loved me. And there was something else, too.

"Noah, you know how we give people gifts?" I said. "Sometimes we have to give something up so that someone else can have it. Like giving the canned food to people without enough to eat?"

"Yeah?" he said.

"Well, I think Jesus loved us so much that he wanted to give us something. Actually, not a *thing*, but himself. That's why he died for us. He gave *himself* up. For us."

"Oh," said Noah. "I think I see what you mean."

"That's a good way of looking at it, Caleb," said Hannah.

We came to the arch that we had gone through yesterday with Jonathan and David. We went under it and walked a little further down the street, talking about Jesus.

We didn't notice the soldiers until one of them stepped right up to us.

"Hey, you, boy!" he said, pointing at me. "Come here!"

Chapter Eight

A Message and More

The soldier stood there, waiting for me to answer.

"What?" I said, suddenly scared. What should I do? I couldn't run away. The soldier would just chase me and he'd get mad. And I couldn't leave Hannah and Noah.

"You are to bring this message to the soldiers stationed on the bakers' street, near the market square." He held out something small and flat.

"B-but I d-don't know where that is," I said. I could hardly speak, I was so scared.

"We are just visitors, sir," said Hannah. "We don't know our way around the city."

"Where are you staying? I will go and get your father to bring the message, then," said the soldier angrily.

Oh no! I thought. We couldn't show them where we were staying. I didn't want to get Jonathan and his family in trouble.

"W-well," I said. "I-I could bring it i-if you tell me how to get there."

"Hmph," said the soldier. He pointed down the street. "It is down that way. Keep going for five or six streets, and turn right at the market—although there is no one selling anything today, as it's the Sabbath. Turn right at the empty square and about one street down is the bakers' street. There are soldiers waiting for this message."

I took the flat thing he gave me. I didn't understand how it was a message. It was like a sandwich of two thin pieces of wood with metal rings connecting them on one side. We turned and started off down the street.

"You! Girl! There is no need to go with him.

Take your little brother back to where you are staying. We do not want people out on the streets today."

Hannah and I looked at each other. She looked as worried and scared as I felt.

"It's okay, Hannah. I think I can find the place all right. I'll be back soon."

"Be careful, Caleb," Hannah whispered, and she ran off toward the house with Noah.

I went the direction the soldier had pointed out. I didn't look back to see if he was watching me or not.

I was afraid I wouldn't know the market square when I saw it, but it was pretty obvious when I got there. It was an open area and I could imagine that it would be full and busy on a market day.

I turned right and started looking for the bakers' street. I had seen how potters and coppersmiths and people like that had workshops with open doors in the front, so people could see them working and buy things. I figured that bakers would have something like that.

Then I remembered that no bakers would

be working on the Sabbath. So now I didn't know how I would recognize the street. There weren't any signs like we have now.

I saw the soldiers before I saw the bakers' street. One of them was standing right at the corner. Another was nearby, talking to a man who looked very nervous.

I went up to the one who wasn't busy. I didn't know what to call him, and I was afraid to say the wrong thing and make him angry.

"Hello, my name is Caleb," I said. "I have a message to give you." I held out the pieces of wood that the other soldier had given me.

"Hello, Caleb," said the soldier. "My name is Quintus. Let me see what important message you bring to us."

This soldier was much younger than the one who had made me run the errand. And he seemed friendly.

He opened the two pieces of wood. The metal rings made it like a book. He looked at it, then lowered it. He had a frown on his face. If he didn't like the message, I hoped he wouldn't be mad at me.

I got a quick look at the "message." It seemed to be written in something soft in a frame of wood on one side. The other piece of wood was like a cover. Quintus took his thumb and rubbed it over the message, making a smooth surface.

"Okay, Caleb. Thank you for this. You can run along now. There is no return message. I need to take a walk out of the city."

"To where, sir?" I asked.

Quintus looked surprised that I would ask. "There is a hill where they do the executions."

"Executions?"

"Yes, where they kill criminals, usually by crucifixion."

Crucifixion? Could this be the place where Jesus had died? Suddenly I wanted to see it. I felt that I would be near him if I could go to the place where he had died.

"Could I come with you, Quintus, sir?" I asked.

"Why do you want to see it? There are no dead bodies—they were taken down yester- day. And actually, it is not to the hill itself that I need to go, but to a nearby garden where they have buried one of the criminals executed yesterday. I must check on the guard there."

"This is my first time here in Jerusalem," I said. "I would like a chance to walk around a little and go outside the city."

"You can come if you like. I do not mind."

We walked along, and he told me about the different parts of the city, the walls around it, and the gates in the walls. A couple times he started to ask about me. I could tell him my age, that my father was a carpenter, and how long I had been in the city, but I didn't want him to ask where I was from.

So I asked him questions instead. He told me about the places he had been stationed, from Rome to Jerusalem.

Eventually we reached the garden. There were three soldiers there. One was standing at attention next to a large rock, and the others were sitting on the ground.

Quintus went up to the one standing and said something. The other answered, and they talked together for a few seconds. Then Quintus turned and walked toward me.

Was this the tomb of Jesus? Quintus had said it was where they had buried someone who had been crucified.

"What was the name of the person who is buried here?" I asked. "Do you know?"

"Yes, his name was Jesus. I heard good things about him and his followers. He taught them to love others, to forgive, to be unselfish. It's too bad. Whatever he did, now he is dead. His followers will be scattered and it will come to nothing."

Come to nothing? I felt as if someone had turned on a very bright light in a dark room. *Come to nothing?*

"No!" I said.

"What?" responded Quintus, surprised.

"It won't come to nothing!" I said. Then, I couldn't help smiling. "It will last forever!"

"What do you mean?"

I couldn't believe I had forgotten! We were so sad to hear Jesus had died that I had almost forgotten what I knew!

I had forgotten that Jesus would rise from the dead!

Chapter Nine

Sharing Plans

"Jesus will rise from the dead, and his followers will continue forever," I said. I felt like laughing, I was so happy.

"So, you are one of them, are you?"

I nodded.

"That is why they have this guard at his tomb," said Quintus. "To prevent his followers from stealing his body and claiming he is alive."

"Thousands of years from now, there will still be followers of Jesus!" I said.

Quintus just shook his head like he didn't believe me, and we walked back toward the city.

I tried hard to pay attention as we walked. I wanted to be able to find my way back there. But my head was filled with so many thoughts that it was hard to focus on where we were going.

Tomorrow! Jesus was going to rise from the dead tomorrow! We could be there. We always went back home after two nights, usually pretty early in the morning. So tonight would be the second night, and we would be able to see Jesus if we got to the tomb before we returned home.

When we got back to where he had been posted, Quintus said, "So, Caleb, can you find your way home from here?"

"Yes, thank you!"

"You are a fine boy, Caleb. Farewell."

I walked off and made the turn at the market square. Then I ran down the street. I couldn't wait to find Hannah and Noah.

When I reached Jonathan's house, I thought

Hannah would be helping Ruth, but Ruth was there by herself.

"Where's Hannah?" I asked.

"She offered to bring the food I prepared to David's mother," said Ruth. "She and little Jacob are doing well!"

"That's great," I said. "Where is Noah, do you know?"

"He went with Rachel and Elizabeth to the upper room at Reuben's house," said Ruth. "They have been gone for a while, but I do not know what they are doing. Here, Caleb, eat some of this before you run off again."

"Oh, later. Thank you! I have to find my brother and sister!"

I found Hannah first, right outside the door. It was a good thing because I thought I was going to burst if I didn't tell someone about Jesus soon.

"Caleb! I'm glad you're back safely. The baby is doing much better now."

"I know—that's great—Hannah, tomorrow! Tomorrow we can see Jesus! He will rise from the dead tomorrow!"

Hannah stared at me with her mouth open, then laughed.

"You're right, Caleb! Everyone has been so sad about what happened that I almost forgot!"

"We have to find Noah!"

"There he is," said Hannah.

Noah and the twins were coming up the street.

"Noah! Come here!" I called, waving frantically to get him to hurry.

"I'll see you later," Noah said to Rachel and Elizabeth.

"Caleb! Hannah!" he said as he ran over to us. "Guess what?"

"Listen, Noah!" I said. "We can see Jesus tomorrow! He will rise from the dead!"

"I know! Rachel and Elizabeth and I were just talking with Mary! She's Jesus's mother. I told her how sad I was that Jesus had died and I didn't get to see him. She smiled at me! And she said, 'You *will* see him.' So I know it will be tomorrow because tomorrow is the third day—it's our last chance."

I told them about going with Quintus to the tomb.

"I *think* I can find my way there. We just have to get up very early."

As we lay down to sleep that night, I thought about our plan. I knew from going to bed on Christmas night that, no matter how awake I felt, there was no way to stay awake all night.

"Hannah, what should we do? How can we make sure we wake up early enough tomorrow?"

"Don't worry," she said. "I will be awake, and I will be sure to wake you, too."

"How can you be sure you will wake up?"

"You see that pitcher on the barrel over by the door?"

"Yeah, what about it?"

"It is used for water. That's what's in the barrel."

"So?" I didn't get why she was telling me this.

"I drank half a pitcher of water a few minutes ago. I will be awake early this morning. Or later tonight. Either one, once I'm awake,

I will not go back to sleep. This is our chance to see Jesus!"

I smiled and shook my head. What a brilliant idea. My sister really was pretty smart, I had to admit.

Chapter Ten

To See Jesus!

Noah said he felt like it was the night before Christmas, too, but he fell asleep almost immediately. I must have fallen asleep soon afterward. It felt like not much time before I felt Hannah shake me.

Hannah, Noah, and I carefully moved toward the door. Hannah had wrapped a loaf of bread in her mantle the night before. We very quietly opened the door and tiptoed out.

It was early in the morning—not light out yet.

We walked quietly but quickly. Noah was

yawning like crazy. He seemed half asleep still. We ate some bread as we walked down the street and under the arch. There was no one around.

I was afraid we might run into soldiers, and then what would I do if they tried to make me run another errand? I thought of cutting through the alleys to avoid them. But I didn't want to risk getting lost. At one point I had to stop. I wasn't sure which way Quintus had turned to go toward the gate.

"I *think* it's this way," I said. Luckily I guessed right, and soon we could see the gate up ahead. The sky was a little bit lighter.

We stopped, though, because we could also see there was a guard standing right at the gate.

"Oh no," said Noah.

"Caleb? Was there a guard on duty when you went out yesterday?" asked Hannah.

"I don't remember," I said. "Wait. Yes, I was with Quintus, and the guard gave a kind of wave to him as we went by. I don't know if they're supposed to stop people or what."

"Caleb, you could do that trick you did last time, in Jericho, when you threw the stone and the robbers heard it and went to see what it was," said Noah.

"That won't work here," I said.

"Well, probably it's easier to walk out of the city than in, right?" said Hannah. "Let's just try to walk calmly by, as if there's no problem, and see what happens."

"Okay, I can't think of anything else to do," I said.

It worked fine. The soldier barely glanced at us. I don't know if it was because we were going out and not coming in, or because we were kids, or what.

From there, I was a little unsure of the way. The paths and gardens and rocky areas looked familiar, but I was not sure of the direction. At one point, we were near a small building that I had never seen before, so we went back and tried a different path.

"Hannah! It's just up ahead. I remember this path!" I whispered. The sky was much lighter.

Noah was more awake now. His eyes were big and round. "I can't believe we are going to see Jesus rise from the dead!"

"Well, we won't see him actually rise from the dead," explained Hannah. "But we hope to see him once he is risen from the dead."

We walked quietly up the path. I knew we were close. We reached a large rock that I remembered being right near the tomb. We peeked around it.

"Teacher!"

We looked just in time to see a woman throw herself down in front of a man in a long white tunic. She hugged his feet.

"It's Mary Magdalene," whispered Hannah.

But I was looking at Jesus. He was standing right there up the path.

"Go tell my brothers," Jesus was saying to her. And she got up and ran off.

Then, Jesus turned and looked over to where we were hiding behind the rock.

"Noah," he said. "Caleb. Hannah."

He said my name!

"Jesus!" Noah yelled. "Jesus!"

"Oh, Jesus, I love you," said Hannah.

I just looked at him. I just looked at his smile that said, *I love you, Caleb.*

"Jesus!" I whispered. "Thank you, Jesus!"

"Go," he said to us. "I send you with my message. Bring it to everyone. Tell everyone of my love."

We started to walk toward him and then to run, but as we ran, the air became thick and heavy and we were running in slow motion, and soon we were back in our house.

We stood looking at each other. And then Noah burst into tears.

Chapter Eleven

Discovering the Secret

Noah sobbed and sobbed.

"Noah," said Hannah. "Don't cry!"

"Noah!" I said. "Why are you crying? That was awesome. We actually got to see Jesus!"

"But I wanted to hug him!" said Noah. "I wanted to talk to him!"

"Oh, Noah," said Hannah, giving him a hug. "You know you can always talk to Jesus—anytime."

Mom and Dad walked into the room just then.

"That's true," said Dad. "But what's wrong with Noah?"

"Nothing!" I said. I didn't want Noah to start telling my parents about going back in time. It would just be too complicated.

Mom looked at me, then Hannah, then Noah. "Does anyone want to tell me why Noah is crying?" she asked.

"Oh, Mom," said Noah. "I just wanted to see Jesus and talk to him. I mean talk to him like I'm talking to you. Not when he's invisible!"

"It's true you can't see him the way we see each other," said Dad. "But you know he is always with us, and always listening."

"I know," said Noah. "I know he is everywhere because he is God."

"And not just that," said Dad. "He's also living inside you."

"What?" I said. "How is he living inside us?"

"Since we are baptized," Mom explained, "we have God's life in us, right? So Jesus, as well as God the Father and their Holy Spirit, is living in us. We can talk to them in our hearts."

"And in heaven, we'll get to see Jesus and talk to him all we want!" said Dad.

"By the way, thank you for collecting these," said Mom. She bent down and picked up a shopping bag.

"Oh, yeah," I said. I had forgotten all about the canned food we were giving to the food drive tomorrow at church. That's what we had been doing when we left two days ago!

"I'll put it in the car so we don't forget it," said Dad, taking the bag from her as they left the room.

"What do you think?" I asked when they were gone. "Do we really have to wait until heaven to see Jesus again?"

"I don't know," said Hannah. "We never did figure out how it happened that we went back in time. So, who knows if it might happen again?"

"Do you think so?" asked Noah, getting excited. "Maybe we could try riding our bikes down the hill!"

"Wait a minute," I said. "Let's try thinking this out."

"Okay," said Hannah. "Let's try to be logical about it. We'll look at each time it happened—what we were doing, and what was different about that time we were doing it."

"Okay, the first time we were riding our bikes down the hill," I said.

"And it was just like what we had done hundreds of times before," said Hannah.

"You never waited for me before, though," said Noah.

"What?" I said.

"When we ride our bikes to that hill, it's always the first one who gets there who goes down first. But that time was different. Both of you waited for me and we went down together."

"That's true," said Hannah. "But we waited for you many times after that, and it never happened again."

Noah shrugged.

"Well, the second time, we jumped off the tree branch together," I said.

"Well, I had never done that before," said Hannah.

"I had—many times," I said. "But it was by myself or with Noah."

"So, the difference was that it was all three of us, right?" asked Noah.

"Yes," I said, thinking a little bit more about it. "But the other different thing was that jumping out of the tree was my idea and you didn't want to do it, Hannah. But I was right and it worked."

Hannah rolled her eyes. "Yes, I admit your idea worked, but we still don't know why."

"The third time we were in the garden, weeding," said Noah.

"Which we don't do very often," said Hannah. "I don't know what was different about that time."

"Maybe because I weeded the tomatoes," said Noah.

Hannah and I both rolled our eyes.

"I don't think that was what did it," I said. "What were we doing the next time?"

"We were walking toward Dad's workshop," said Noah. "He wanted us to try out the new 3-D puzzle he was working on."

"That's right," said Hannah. "And there was nothing special about that. We've walked between the house and the workshop millions of times—alone and together."

I was just about to agree, but I remembered something.

"You know, there was something different. Right before that, I was walking to Dad's workshop by myself," I said. "Dad had texted Mom that he wanted the three of us to come over. I went out the kitchen door and saw you coming from the garden. I almost didn't say anything because I just wanted to go help Dad by myself."

"You and Noah are always trying to leave me out when Dad wants us to try out new toys. You say they're for boys, which is not even true," said Hannah.

"You always say the oldest should get to be first," said Noah. "That's why we don't want you to come!"

"What?" said Hannah. "I do not. You

always get to go first because you're the youngest!"

"Wait!" I said. "Wait! Stop fighting. I just thought of something."

"What?" said Hannah, still frowning.

"Noah, remember what you said about when we rode down the hill together?"

"It was the first time you waited for me?" he said.

"Right. That was nice of us, wasn't it? We didn't really want to wait," I said, and I smiled because I really knew I had discovered the secret. "And Hannah, you didn't really want to climb the tree and jump off with us, did you? It was hot and you just wanted to sit in the shade and read your book."

"True," she said. "What about it?"

"And *none* of us wanted to weed the garden. We were trying to think of excuses, but we decided to do it because Mom asked us to," I continued.

"Oh!" said Hannah and Noah at the same time. They were staring at me with their mouths open.

"You get it?" I said. "It must be something about when we do something nice even though we don't feel like it!"

"Oh, you're a genius, Caleb!" said Hannah. "That's it! It has always happened when we did something nice, something generous. It's when we act generously instead of selfishly!"

"Like the other time," said Noah, "Hannah and I said we'd stay inside and help you with your turn to watch Garrett, even though we all wanted to be outside, right?"

"Yes!" I said. "And then this time, you and I gave the last cans of ravioli for the poor, like Hannah said we should, even though we were planning on eating them for lunch. That was generous, right?"

"So, that's the secret?" said Noah. "You figured it out?"

"Yes, it all fits," said Hannah. "It must be that. It's amazing that we never saw the similarities before." She stopped and laughed. "Remember how we all tried to roll down the hill?"

She and Noah were laughing, but I was still thinking. Something wasn't right.

"Oh! Hannah!" I said. "Now the whole thing is ruined."

"What? What are you talking about, Caleb? You're a genius. You solved the mystery."

"Yeah, I know, but now it's ruined. How can we do something we *don't* feel like doing when we actually *will* feel like doing it because we want to go back in time?"

Hannah and Noah looked at me.

"What?" said Noah.

"I see what you mean," said Hannah. "It won't be generous because we'll be hoping to get something out of it—to have another adventure. So it won't work."

"That's why it didn't work to all go down the hill on our bikes, after the first time," I said.

"I think you're right. It wasn't hard—it wasn't a sacrifice to wait for each other because we all wanted to try it."

"Well, it will make us think when there's something we don't feel like doing," said Noah.

"And you never know. Maybe it will work again someday."

"Maybe," I said. But I didn't think it would. I thought our adventures were over—at least that kind of adventure. For sure there would be other kinds.

Chapter Twelve

Giving the Gift

The next day was Sunday and I thought it was just a regular one, but I realized it wasn't as soon as we got into church. For one thing, there were huge bunches of flowers around the altar in the sanctuary. Then when the music started at the beginning of Mass, there were *trumpets* playing with the organ and the choir. And the song was really exciting! It was all about victory, with lots of "alleluias" in it. Then, in the entrance procession, I saw Father Joe was wearing white, instead of green like he's been wearing for months.

Well, it turned out that it was the feast of Christ the King. I never remembered hearing about it before, but I guess I did last year and just forgot. Or maybe I wasn't paying attention. Anyway, the music was great, and during the readings, there was other stuff about kings and kingdoms.

"I didn't know Jesus was a king," Noah whispered to me as we sat down after the readings.

I was confused, too. I knew Jesus worked as a carpenter. I knew he was a "Good Shepherd" because he guides us and takes care of us. I knew he was a teacher and a friend, especially of children. I knew he is God and can do miracles and everything. But I never thought he was a king. He was poor and worked hard. He didn't have a palace and servants to do everything for him. Also, he loved everyone and did things for them, but a lot of kings I had heard about bossed people around.

I was hoping Father Joe would explain it during his homily. He did!

"Isn't it strange," said Father Joe, "that on a feast called Christ the King, the Gospel reading refers to Jesus's passion and death? The reading is a conversation between Jesus and Pontius Pilate, the Roman governor. Jesus is on trial. In the part of the story after this reading, Pilate hands Jesus over to be crucified.

"The reason we hear this reading on this feast is to help us understand what we mean by 'Christ the King.' Jesus is King of the universe— he is in charge. He rules over everything and everyone. But he is a completely different kind of king. He's a king who serves us. He's a poor king. And, the most amazing thing is that he's a king who loves us so much he died for us."

Noah and I looked at each other and smiled.

"And that's what the Mass is all about," continued Father Joe. "It's a memorial of Jesus's death and resurrection. And in a real, sacramental way, Jesus's passion, death, resurrection, and ascension into heaven are present here and now. We can't build a time machine to go back and be there when Jesus died and rose to life. But when we are here at Mass,

Jesus is offering himself and *we are there*."

Wow! I had never thought of the Mass that way before!

"But it's not enough," continued Father Joe, "to just be present. We can't just sit there and watch. It's not like watching a football game. We have been *baptized*. That means we belong to Jesus. We are members of his body. We are supposed to participate!

"And how do we participate? We offer *ourselves* along with Jesus. We offer all we are and have. And he takes our little offering and joins it with his saving death and resurrection."

Wow, Jesus! I prayed. *I'm so happy to know that you are my king, too. I want to belong to you always! Thank you for inventing this way for us to be with you in the Mass. I'm not sure what I have to offer you. You give me yourself when I receive Holy Communion. So, I want to give you myself—like Father Joe said—everything I am and everything I have. Because I love you and I want to be with you always.*

Where Is It
in the Bible?

The story Jonathan told about the man carrying the water jar is in the Gospels according to Mark and Luke. Here is the way Mark tells the story:

On the first day of Unleavened Bread, when the Passover lamb is sacrificed, his disciples said to him, "Where do you want us to go and make the preparations for you to eat the Passover?" So he sent two of his disciples, saying to them, "Go into the city, and a man carrying a jar of water will meet you; follow him, and wherever he enters, say to the owner of the house, 'The Teacher asks, Where is my guest room where I may eat the Passover with my disciples?' He will show you a large room upstairs, furnished and ready. Make preparations for us there." So the disciples set out and went to the city, and found everything as he had told them; and they prepared the Passover meal (Mark 14:12–16).

David talks about being in the Temple with his father, and hearing Jesus teaching. This little story is also included in two of the Gospels. Here it is as told in the Gospel according to Mark:

[Jesus] sat down opposite the treasury, and watched the crowd putting money into the treasury. Many rich people put in large sums. A poor widow came and put in two small copper coins, which are worth a penny. Then he called his disciples and said to them, "Truly I tell you, this poor widow has put in more than all those who are contributing to the treasury" (Mark 12:41–43).

Each of the Gospels tells the stories of those who saw Jesus after he rose from the dead.

Here is the story of Mary Magdalene meeting Jesus, as told in the Gospel according to John:

> But Mary stood weeping outside the tomb. As she wept, she bent over to look into the tomb; and she saw two angels in white, sitting where the body of Jesus had been lying, one at the head and the other at the feet. They said to her, "Woman, why are you weeping?" She said to them, "They have taken away my Lord, and I do not know where they have laid him." When she had said this, she turned around and saw Jesus standing there, but she did not know that it was Jesus. Jesus said to her, "Woman, why are you weeping? Whom are you looking for?" Supposing him to be the gardener, she said to him, "Sir, if you have carried him away, tell me where you have laid him, and I will take him away." Jesus said to her, "Mary!" She turned and said to him in Hebrew, "Rabbouni!" (which means Teacher). Jesus said to her, "Do not hold on to me, because I have not yet ascended to the Father. But go to my brothers and say

to them, 'I am ascending to my Father and your Father, to my God and your God.'" Mary Magdalene went and announced to the disciples, "I have seen the Lord"; and she told them that he had said these things to her (John 20:11–18).

Gospel TimeTrekkers

Three ordinary kids, six extraordinary adventures, one incredible quest!

Join Caleb, Hannah, and Noah as they're whisked away to the time of Jesus and find themselves immersed in some of the most amazing Bible stories of all!

Written by Maria Grace Dateno, FSP
Illustrated by Paul Cunningham

Who are the Daughters of St. Paul?

We are Catholic sisters. Our mission is to be like Saint Paul and tell everyone about Jesus! There are so many ways for people to communicate with each other. We want to use all of them so everyone will know how much God loves us. We do this by printing books (you're holding one!), making radio shows, singing, helping people at our bookstores, using the Internet, and in many other ways.

Visit our Web site at www.pauline.org

BOOKS & MEDIA

The Daughters of St. Paul operate book and media centers at the following addresses. Visit, call, or write the one nearest you today, or find us at www.paulinestore.org.

CALIFORNIA

3908 Sepulveda Blvd, Culver City, CA 90230 — 310-397-8676
3250 Middlefield Road, Menlo Park, CA 94025 — 650-369-4230

FLORIDA

145 S.W. 107th Avenue, Miami, FL 33174 — 305-559-6715

HAWAII

1143 Bishop Street, Honolulu, HI 96813 — 808-521-2731

ILLINOIS

172 North Michigan Avenue, Chicago, IL 60601 — 312-346-4228

LOUISIANA

4403 Veterans Memorial Blvd, Metairie, LA 70006 — 504-887-7631

MASSACHUSETTS

885 Providence Hwy, Dedham, MA 02026 — 781-326-5385

MISSOURI

9804 Watson Road, St. Louis, MO 63126 — 314-965-3512

NEW YORK

64 W. 38th Street, New York, NY 10018 — 212-754-1110

SOUTH CAROLINA

243 King Street, Charleston, SC 29401 — 843-577-0175

TEXAS

Currently no book center; for parish exhibits or outreach evangelization, contact: 210-569-0500, or SanAntonio@paulinemedia.com, or P.O. Box 761416, San Antonio, TX 78245

VIRGINIA

1025 King Street, Alexandria, VA 22314 — 703-549-3806

CANADA

3022 Dufferin Street, Toronto, ON M6B 3T5 — 416-781-9131

¡También somos su fuente para libros,
videos y música en español!